FRIGHTFUL FAMILIES

D1635389

For Hannah and Holly Powell – worth a million.

S.M.

For Katie.

T.M.

ORCHARD BOOKS
96 Leonard Street, London EC2A 4XD
Orchard Books Australia
Level 17/207 Kent Street, Sydney, NSW 2000
ISBN 1 84362 565 2 (hardback)
ISBN 1 84362 573 3 (paperback)
First published in Great Britain in 2005
First paperback publication in 2006
Text © Sue Mongredien 2005
Illustrations © Teresa Murfin 2005
The rights of Sue Mongredien to be identified as the author
and of Teresa Murfin to be identified as the illustrator of this work
have been asserted by them in accordance with the
Copyright, Designs and Patents Act, 1988.
A CIP catalogue record for this book is available
from the British Library.
1 3 5 7 9 10 8 6 4 2 (hardback)
1 3 5 7 9 10 8 6 4 2 (paperback)
Printed in Great Britain
www.wattspublishing.co.uk

MILLIONAIRE MAYHEM

SUE MONGREDIEN • TERESA MURFIN

ORCHARD BOOKS

Zoe and Zach Fourleaf lived with their mum and dad at 45 Drizzle Terrace. It was a small house, with a falling-apart roof, a cracked kitchen window and a mud-patch for a garden. But it was home.

Then, one evening, everything changed.
"1...6...18...37...40...45..." boomed
a voice from the TV.

"The jackpot is an estimated twenty
million pounds tonight. We think there's just
one lucky winner!"

Zoe looked up from her comic, and stared at the television. Had she heard that right? "Zach, where's the lottery ticket?" she asked.

Zach saw the numbers on the screen, and gulped. "Our birthday's on the first," he said.

Zoe nodded. "And Dad's is on the sixth."

"Mum's birthday is on the eighteenth, and she's thirty-seven," Zach added, turning pale.

"Dad's forty..." Zoe stuttered.

"...And we live at number 45," they said together. They turned and stared at each other. "We're millionaires!" they screamed.

Life went very weird after that. First,
a smart-suited lady from the lottery came
to Drizzle Terrace to check the ticket.

"Congratulations," she told Mrs Fourleaf.
"You're now officially rich!"

Then the whole family had their photo taken for the local newspaper.

FOURLEAFS ARE IN CLOVER blared the headlines the next day.

That weekend, Mr and Mrs Fourleaf threw a huge street party to celebrate. There was music from the Drizzle Terrace Stompers, fish and chips from the Drizzle Terrace Friers, and dancing led by old Granny Greenfield, who taught them the hand-jive.

And then, when the millionaire-making cheque arrived, the Fourleaf family went shopping. As a postman and a school dinner-lady, Mr and Mrs Fourleaf had never had much spare cash. Now that they were rich, they wanted to shop their socks off.

Zoe chose twenty pairs of trainers, sixteen
bags, eight swimming costumes, fifteen
pairs of jeans, fourteen skirts, twelve tops,
a leather jacket, a denim jacket, a fake-fur
bomber jacket, roller skates, glittery hair gel,
nail varnish, and a mini trampoline.

Zach chose a mountain bike, fifty-eight computer games, a shelf-load of CDs, a stereo system, a pool table, five new footballs, a micro-scooter and a ping pong table.

Mr and Mrs Fourleaf bought themselves
new watches, designer clothes and
top-of-the-range cars.

And on the way home, they spotted
a twenty-bedroom mansion with its own
swimming pool. It was for sale.

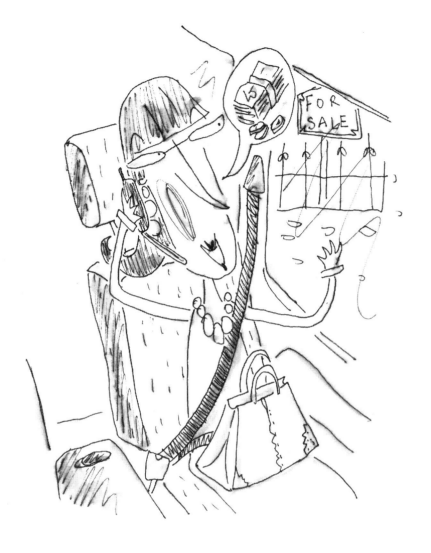

Mrs Fourleaf pulled out her new mobile phone and called the estate agent. "We'll buy it," she declared. "Cash."

"Move house?" Zoe gasped.

"Leave Drizzle Terrace?" gaped Zach.

"Of course!" cried Mr Fourleaf, slapping the steering wheel. "Millionaires live in mansions, don't they? Everyone knows that!"

"We'll need extra space for all our new things!" Mrs Fourleaf beamed.

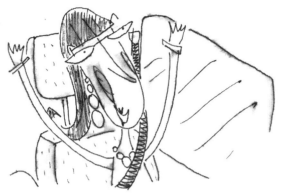

Zach bit his lip. Zoe scratched her head. They hadn't thought about moving house.

"Just think," Mrs Fourleaf went on brightly, "you can have your own bedrooms now, plus a games room with Zach's pool table and some pinball machines, a ballroom for parties, a gym, a stable for Zoe's ponies, and lots of rooms for guests..."

Zach loved the sound of the games room...

Zoe couldn't wait to see the stable.

"OK," they chorused. "When do
we move?"

After a spectacular send-off party with fish and chips all round, where the Drizzle Terrace Stompers played their best tunes, and old Granny Greenfield taught everybody the samba, the Fourleafs moved out of Drizzle Terrace.

Moving to the mansion was wonderful at first. Zoe adored her ponies...

And Zach loved his football pitch.

Mrs Fourleaf took flying lessons in a private jet.

And Mr Fourleaf bought a miniature train that he drove around the gardens. And they still hadn't finished shopping.

The kids at school thought it was cool that Zach and Zoe's parents were spending their money on such extraordinary things. But Zach and Zoe were starting to find it a bit embarrassing.

Being millionaires had sent their parents potty!

Zach wished Mrs Fourleaf wouldn't pick them up from school in her pink sports car. All the boys in his class had started making jokes about it.

And Zoe wished Mr Fourleaf would stop riding his racehorse past school and waving at her. The headteacher didn't like that at all. He liked it even less when he slipped on something that the horse had left behind.

"All this awful stuff," Zoe complained to Zach one day. She kicked the marble statue of a moose Mr Fourleaf had bought for the back garden.

"I know. And now school is a nightmare, too," Zach moaned, eyeing the sour-faced stone sphinx by the pond.

Just then, their parents came outside. "Great news!" Mr Fourleaf cried. "You're leaving school!"

"Yey!" cheered Zach and Zoe.

Mrs Fourleaf beamed. "Meet your new governess, Miss Gorgon," she said.

A tall woman with a flinty gaze stepped out of the house. Zach and Zoe stopped cheering at once. Suddenly, things had gone from bad to worse...

Miss Gorgon was every bit as awful as she looked. She taught them Greek and Latin every day and gave them piles of homework. She never joked. She never praised them for hard work. She never even read them any good stories.

After lessons, the Hartley-Foxtrot children would come over to play. They lived down the road and were rip-roaringly rich. They were also spectacular show-offs. "Mummy took us to Buckingham Palace for lunch at the weekend," Lucinda would simper to Zoe. "It was super-*dooper.*"

"I say, Zachary, old boy, have you seen Daddy's new Ferrari?" Archibald would swank. "Totally turbo!"

Sometimes in the evening, Mr and Mrs
Fourleaf held parties, but these were
different, too. Forget the Drizzle Terrace
Stompers – they hired a ten-piece orchestra
in the ballroom instead.

Ballgowns and dinner jackets were worn – even by the children. And instead of fish and chips, the guests ate yucky caviar and quail's eggs. Granny Greenfield wasn't even invited.

Zoe was starting to wish they hadn't won the money. She didn't feel like her life was any better than it had been before. In fact, it was a whole lot worse.

"Sometimes I hate being a millionaire," she confessed to Zach one evening.

Zach nodded. "Me, too," he said. "The Hartley-Foxtrots are vile, Miss Gorgon is evil and Mum and Dad are just...bonkers."

Zoe and Zach were silent for a moment.

"I wonder how much money they've got left," Zach said thoughtfully.

"Maybe if we helped them spend the rest of it, everything would go back to normal," Zoe answered. "And we'd move back to Drizzle Terrace and all our friends."

Zach nodded. "Exactly. All we have to do is think of some ways to blow the rest of the winnings!" he said. "No problem!"

The next day, Zach persuaded Mrs Fourleaf to donate ten thousand pounds to a donkey sanctuary. But then their accountant phoned five minutes later to say that their savings had earned twenty thousand pounds in interest.

The day after, Zoe talked Mr Fourleaf into
buying an expensive helicopter – but then
a letter arrived saying that the shares they'd
bought in a diamond company had tripled in
value, earning them a cool million.

Then, when work began on the Fourleafs'
new garden, the head gardener dug up some
priceless Roman remains. A team of
archaeologists were brought in.

"If these remains are as valuable as we think they are, you're going to be very rich!" one archaeologist joked to Zoe.

"Great," she sighed miserably. "Just what we didn't want."

Mrs Fourleaf was so excited, she managed to crash her helicopter into the town hall.

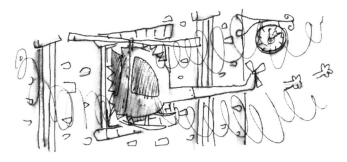

Nobody was hurt, but the story was all over the newspapers. Zach and Zoe had never felt so embarrassed.

"We've GOT to go for broke," Zoe groaned. "Mum and Dad are out of control!"

That afternoon, the twins had their PE lesson. "Run round the house three times," Miss Gorgon barked as usual. "Go!"

Zoe and Zach had both loved PE at school – Zach had been a star footballer, and Zoe had been the best gymnast. But running around their house was really boring!

"Come on," Zach whispered. "I've got an idea."

Zoe followed Zach into Mr Fourleaf's engine shed. "Let's take the train around instead of running," he said with a grin.

Zoe burst out laughing. "Nice one," she said. "Do you know how to work it?"

Zach stepped up into the cab. "No worries," he said, pointing to an ignition key. "I just turn this and..."

CHUG-CHUG-CHUG-CHUG-CHUG!

"We're off!" he yelled. "Hold tight!"

The train started along the tracks. "Tally-ho!" Zoe giggled. "Look, Miss Gorgon's seen us," she laughed.

A figure was charging towards them, shaking a bony fist. "Get off that train!" she shrieked.

"Miss Gorgon's doing the running for us!" Zach chuckled.

"She's on the track!" Zoe cried. "Stop the train, Zach!"

Zach gulped suddenly and stared blankly at the control panel. "Er...*how*?"

The next morning, the Fourleafs were sitting down to breakfast when the call came.

"Do you want the bad news or the even worse news first?" Mr Fourleaf said glumly, clicking off the gold-plated phone.

"Don't tell me the helicopter is a write-off?" Mrs Fourleaf asked, clapping a hand to her mouth in dismay.

Mr Fourleaf shook his head. "Worse," he said. "Miss Gorgon has resigned. Her lawyer says she's claiming damages for trauma. She thinks it'll take her years to recover from the shock of having to throw herself out of the way of a speeding train."

"It was hardly speeding," Zoe snorted. "It only goes at five miles an hour!"

Zach rolled his eyes. "And we only ran over her *handbag*," he said scornfully.

"Well, she says she's traumatised," Mr Fourleaf said. "She's suing us for millions."

Mrs Fourleaf dropped her fork with a clatter. "No," she breathed.

Mr Fourleaf nodded. "Yes," he said. "Afraid so." He turned to the twins. "Sorry, kids," he said, "but it looks like we're poor again."

Zach and Zoe couldn't hide their smiles. "Actually, Dad," Zoe said, "we don't mind all that much."

"We miss our old home," Zach went on. "And our friends," Zoe added. "Even school," Zach confessed.

Zoe took a deep breath. "Most of all, though," she said, "we miss you two."

Mr and Mrs Fourleaf blinked again. "Us?" they replied.

Zach nodded. "You haven't seemed like Mum and Dad lately," he said. "You've just seemed like...millionaires."

"The helicopter and the train and the pink sports car... We felt a bit embarrassed about it all actually," said Zoe.

Mrs Fourleaf looked dazed. "I thought you were happy being millionaires," she said.

"You made us happy when you were a dinner lady, Mum, and organised streeet parties for everyone," said Zoe.

"Admit it, Dad," said Zach, "those ballroom dancers aren't a patch on Granny Greenfield."

Mr Fourleaf smiled. "Now you mention it," he said, "I've missed the old dear, too."

And so, just a few weeks later, the Fourleaf family moved house again. Not back to Drizzle Terrace, as the twins had hoped, but to a slightly bigger house just two roads away. There was no swimming pool or stable or gym, but the garden was big enough for a football net and it was near their old school, and their friends too.

Lots of the Fourleafs' new purchases had to go. The sports cars, private jet and railway were auctioned. The ponies and pool table were sold, too.

"I can't wait for things to get back to normal," Zoe said.

"No more Miss Gorgon, or yucky food," Zach agreed in relief.

Mr and Mrs Fourleaf walked over to the twins. "I know it's been hard giving all this up," Mr Fourleaf said to them. "That's why we felt we couldn't sell *everything*."

Mrs Fourleaf put an arm around Zoe. "We're taking our favourite things with us," she said.

"You mean, we're keeping the ponies after all?" Zoe burst out excitedly.

"And my sound system?" Zach added in the next breath.

Mr Fourleaf smiled proudly. "Oh, better than those," he said. "We'll show our new neighbours that we're not just ordinary people. Look!"

Zach and Zoe watched as a small crane was driven to the front of the house. And then, to their horror, it slowly heaved up the sphinx from the ground.

"The sphinx is coming with us?" Zoe asked in dismay.

"Oh yes," Mr Fourleaf said. "And the moose statue."

"And the tiger-print sofa," Mrs Fourleaf smiled. "All of our nicest things!"

Zoe didn't know whether to laugh or cry. From the look on Zach's face, he wasn't sure either. "Well," she said. "You're right about one thing. There's no chance our neighbours will think that we're ordinary people."

Zach caught her eye, and they both started to laugh. "No danger whatsoever," he spluttered. He grinned at his extraordinary parents. "Shall we go?"

FRIGHTFUL FAMILIES

WRITTEN BY SUE MONGREDIEN • ILLUSTRATED BY TERESA MURFIN

Explorer Trauma	1 84362 571 7
Headmaster Disaster	1 84362 572 5
Millionaire Mayhem	1 84362 573 3
Clown Calamity	1 84362 574 1
Popstar Panic	1 84362 575 X
Football-mad Dad	1 84362 576 8
Chef Shocker	1 84362 577 6
Astronerds	1 84362 803 1

All priced at £3.99

Frightful Families are available from all good book shops, or can be ordered
direct from the publisher: Orchard Books, PO BOX 29, Douglas IM99 1BQ
Credit card orders please telephone 01624 836000
or fax 01624 837033 or visit our Internet site: www.wattspub.co.uk
or e-mail: bookshop@enterprise.net for details.

To order please quote title, author and ISBN
and your full name and address.
Cheques and postal orders should be made payable to 'Bookpost plc.'
Postage and packing is FREE within the UK
(overseas customers should add £1.00 per book).
Prices and availability are subject to change.